Casper the Caterpillar

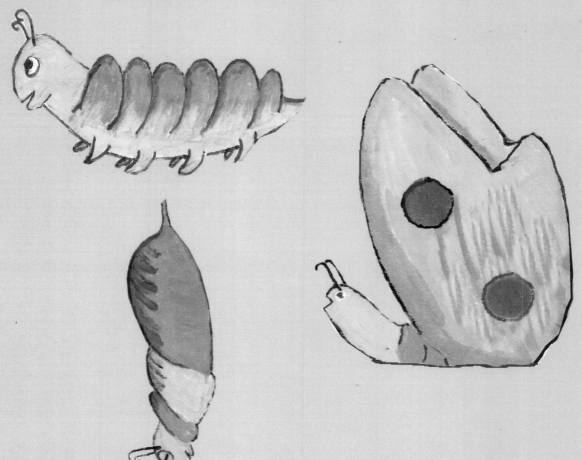

Casper the Caterpillar

by

Sandra Stoner-Mitchell

Dedication

I would like to dedicate this book to some very special people

Eric Stoner
Ellie Mitchell
Scout Mitchell
Sofie Buckley
Chloe Stoner
Maisie Sherin

You are all the reason I need to continue writing childrens books

Lots of love,
Sandra xxx

Casper the Caterpillar

**Casper was a caterpillar sitting
on a leaf,**

**He looked all around it, then he
looked underneath,**

**He called out for his mummy
but she was not around,**

**So with a little wiggle he jiggled
to the ground**

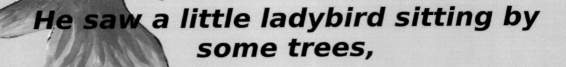

He saw a little ladybird sitting by
some trees,

And went across and said to her
"Could you help me, please?

I can't find my mummy, do you know
where she might be?"

The ladybird said "Sorry, she hasn't
been past me."

Then Casper saw a little frog on a lily pad

And went across and said to him "I am very sad,

I can't find my mummy, do you know where she might be?"

The little frog said "Sorry, she hasn't been past me."

Casper walked on further and saw
some buzzing bees,

He went across and said to one
"Could you help me please?

I can't find my mummy, do you know
where she might be?"

The buzzing bee said "Sorry, she
hasn't been past me."

Casper saw a pretty snail
cleaning out her home,

He went across and said to her
"I am all alone,

I can't find my mummy, do you
know where she might be?"

The pretty snail said "Sorry!
She hasn't been past me."

Then Casper spied a spider just
finishing his tea,

He went across and said to him
"Please can you help me?

I can't find my mummy, do you
know where she might be?"

But the spider said "Sorry! She
hasn't been past me."

Now Casper was quite tired, he'd walked a long, long way,

"I can't stop because I've got to find my mum today.

I've asked so many creatures, do you know where she might be?"

But everyone said "Sorry! She hasn't been past me!"

Casper found a nice big leaf, he thought he'd have a doze,

He fell asleep and while he slept something strange arose,

His little caterpillar shape became a chrysalis,

So when he wakes, he'll be surprised, and wonder what he is!

Then Casper woke and saw his
wings, he was a butterfly!

And all at once he saw his mum as
she came flying by.

And all the creatures he had asked
where his mum might be,

Came and shouted really loud,
"Yes, she's been past me!"

Other books by Sandra Stoner-Mitchell

For Children

The Hedgerow Capers Series

Hedgerow Capers

The Day Before Christmas Eve

The Fun Begins

A Spot of Bother

For Adults

A Collection of Short Stories

Spiritual Moments

About

Sandra Stoner-Mitchell was born in Ipswich, Suffolk but spent most of her life in the South of England. She lived in Spain for several years with her husband, learning the language and writing but they have now moved back to the South of England.

Sandra began writing short stories and poems at an early age but has only recently started having her work published.
She has written a whole series of books for children about The Hedgerow Gang in the Hedgerow Capers Series of books.

Sandra has also written two books for adults.
You can find out more about Sandra and her books on her website and Facebook. You can also follow her on Twitter.

http://sandrascapers.com

https://www.facebook.com/hedgerowvillagecapers

https://twitter.com/hedgerowcapers